Pulling THE Lion's Tail

BY JANE KURTZ

ILLUSTRATED BY FLOYD COOPER

SIMON & SCHUSTER BOOKS FOR YOUNG READERS

To Angie and Preston

—J.K.

For Dayton C.

—F.C.

SIMON & SCHUSTER BOOKS FOR YOUNG READERS
1230 Avenue of the Americas
New York, New York 10020
Text copyright © 1995 by Jane Kurtz
Illustrations copyright © 1995 by Floyd Cooper
All rights reserved including the right of
reproduction in whole or in part in any form.
SIMON & SCHUSTER BOOKS FOR YOUNG READERS
is a trademark of Simon & Schuster.
Book design by Lucille Chomowicz
The text for this book is set in Aldus.
The illustrations were done in oils.
Manufactured in the United States of America
10 9 8 7 6 5 4 3 2 1
Library of Congress Cataloging-in-Publication Data
Kurtz, Jane.
   Pulling the lion's tail / by Jane Kurtz ; illustrated by
Floyd Cooper.
      p.   cm.
   Summary: Her grandfather finds a clever way to help an
impatient young Ethiopian girl get to know her father's new wife.
   [1. Ethiopia—Fiction.   2. Stepmothers—Fiction.
   3. Patience—Fiction.   4. Grandfathers—Fiction.]
   I. Cooper, Floyd, ill.   II. Title.
PZ7.K9626Pu 1995 [E]—dc20   93-22836
ISBN: 0-689-80324-9

Author's Note

I would like to thank Aster Dibaba, a longtime friend of my family's, for helping me understand what life might be like for an Ethiopian child with a new stepmother. In Ethiopian society, respect for elders is considered to be almost the most important thing every child needs to learn. Aster told me that a new stepmother would not only be shy and perhaps a little homesick, but would also doubtless hear from her new husband that she must take care to make her new stepchildren respect her. Using the plot of a traditional Ethiopian folktale, I then was able to tell the story of how one girl, longing for love, finds great patience.

In the high mountains of Ethiopia there once lived a girl named Almaz. Every night when the sun stooped low over the hills, she waited at the door, hopping first on one foot and then the other, until her father came home and lit the long beeswax candle on the pole in the middle of the room. Then she rushed to him and poured the water for his hands and brought him the peppery stew called *wat* that her grandmother had sent over and the *injera*, the thin bread she herself had cooked.

"Is it good?" she asked every night as he ate.

"It is good," he said every night, even though she knew she should have let the batter sit for a few more days. But when he smiled, she hid her burnt fingers and hoped that tomorrow her *injera* would taste like the *injera* her mother used to make.

Later, after she, too, had eaten and her father had blown out the candle, she lay in the darkness and remembered. Sometimes she remembered her mother's face. And sometimes she remembered the night her mother died, when the weeper came in to sing a long sorrowful song, and the mourners gathered around her and cried, "*Waye, waye*," and Almaz took off her rings and her necklace, and her hair was cut short.

All that long year, Almaz and her father wore black clothing and faces like the rain. Then one day her father came to her. "The days of the big rains are coming," he said, "so tomorrow I am going to a village far from here. I will bring back a new wife."

Next morning Almaz ran to the marketplace. When she saw her grandfather, wisest of all the village elders, sitting under a tree, she ran to him and kissed his hand three times. "Good days are ahead," she said. "Soon I will have a new mother. And the big rains are coming to bring us food. When will they begin?"

Her grandfather closed his eyes and sat silently. Finally he said, "Much of what is good comes slowly."

But Almaz had already run off.

For days after her father's announcement, the house was full of people. Almaz's aunts and cousins and grandmother moved in and out, in and out, preparing the wedding feast.

Almaz moved in and out, in and out, asking questions. "Will my new mother be kind?"

But her grandmother, with tears in her eyes from chopping onions, said, "*Shhh*, Almaz. Get us some more water from the stream."

Almaz went, but she paused by the door. "Will my new mother be young or old?" she asked one of her aunts.

"*Shhh*," said her aunt. "Don't be disrespectful."

Finally the day of the feast came, and loaves of bread were laid on beds of green branches. "They're coming!" called one of the cousins, running up the path.

All the women cried, "*Lei, lei, lei,*" and Almaz started for the door; but her grandmother said, "Almaz, Almaz, blow up the fire."

So she stooped by the fire and watched and saw her new mother come in with her eyes down.

All night long the guests feasted. "May I go to my father?" Almaz asked her grandmother and cousins and aunts, but everybody said, "No, no," so she sulked and watched through a crack in the wall. When it was her turn to dance and play the drum, Almaz tried to see her new mother's face, but it was hidden in shadow.

Days later, when all the guests were gone, Almaz's father called her over. "Kibret is your new mother," he said. "Although she is young, you must respect her and do as she says."

Kibret kissed Almaz on both cheeks but did not look up.

Next morning and every morning after, Almaz brought water from the stream. Then her father sent her out to watch the cows and feed the chickens and grind the corn and chop the wood. At night, when the sun stooped over the hills, she came inside.

From the shadows she watched Kibret pour the water for her father's hands and serve the *wat* and *injera*. Then Kibret would sit and eat tiny bites, and after they were finished she would bring the water and the food for Almaz.

Once when Kibret was pouring the water for her hands, Almaz said, "May I see the new things you got for your wedding?"

But Kibret looked down and said nothing, so Almaz did not ask again.

One morning in the middle of rainy season, Almaz ran out of the house. The chickens flapped and squawked in a wild commotion. Almaz ran through the flock, scattering feathers.

Up, up, up the road she walked, faster and faster, to her grandfather's hut. When she got to the door, she stopped. But she didn't wait for her grandfather, the wisest elder, to say welcome. She bent her head and stepped in through the doorway.

Outside, the sun was bright and sharp.

Inside, the hut was cool and dark.

"Sit down," said her grandfather in a silky old voice.

But Almaz was too impatient to sit. Without waiting for her eyes to grow used to the dark, she spoke. "My new mother never talks to me," she said. "She never says good morning."

"I'm over here," her grandfather said.

Almaz turned around. "She doesn't even look at me," she said. "She doesn't love me."

Her grandfather sat and thought.

Almaz hopped on one foot and then the other. She listened in the cool silence for as long as she could. Then she turned to go.

Just then her grandfather spoke. "I will tell you the secret to winning your new mother's love," he said.

"What?" Almaz said. "What?"

"But first," her grandfather said, "you must bring me something."

"Only tell me what," Almaz said. "I will bring anything."

"Bring me some hair from the tail of a lion," said her grandfather.

Going home, Almaz walked so fast that dust swirled up around her. "Hair from a lion," she said. "Impossible."

She chopped some wood and ground some corn and went inside.

Kibret was spinning thread without a word.

Almaz watched as Kibret worked the thin thread smooth with her fingers. When the spindle was full, Kibret put it in the corner and knelt by the fire. Almaz remembered her mother's face and was sad. "All right," Almaz said to herself. "I'll try."

In the morning Almaz took a piece of salty dried meat from a bag over the fire and wrapped it in a fat false banana leaf. She marched as fast as she could to the lion's cave. As she got closer, she walked slower. By the time she reached the eucalyptus tree near the cave, she was creeping.

With tiny baby steps, she inched up to the cave.

Something inside the cave snorted.

"*Ayaiee*," Almaz shouted. She threw down the meat and ran all the way home.

That night, as she sat by the fire, she said to Kibret, "Why does your *injera* taste better than when I made it?"

"Look," said Kibret, pointing at bubbles in the batter. "The *injera* has eyes. That's how you know you have given your batter the time it needs." But she did not look at Almaz as she spoke.

Next day Almaz took another piece of meat. Laying each foot down as softly as a falling leaf, she walked up to the cave. Then she threw down the meat and ran.

But this time she ran only as far as the eucalyptus tree. Behind its slender trunk, she watched the lion eat the meat.

She brought meat for many days.

At first she could not bear to look at the lion, with its wild red mouth and careless teeth.

But after many days she grew braver.

One day when she took meat to the lion, she did not throw it down and run behind the tree. She crept one step toward the lion. The next day she crept closer still. Finally, one day she stood right beside the meat, trembling because the lion's breath smelled of death, but she did not run away.

After many weeks Almaz came to like going to the lion's cave. The lion grunted and sometimes purred with a slow, secret smile.

At home, whenever Almaz remembered the purring, she did not mind the silence so much. One time, she even sat by Kibret as her stepmother wove a basket. "Your fingers are very beautiful," Almaz said.

Kibret looked at her in surprise. Then she showed Almaz how to weave a little, but their hands did not touch.

The next time she visited the lion, it was easy for Almaz to put her hand on his tail as he chewed.

She held her breath. She tugged one strand of hair.

The lion kept eating.

Almaz gently pulled a little more hair, ready to run.

The lion didn't even look at her.

All the way back to the village, Almaz filled her hands with Maskal daisies that come with the big rains. When she reached her house, she put the flowers at Kibret's feet and took down the drum and played a rhythm of triumph.

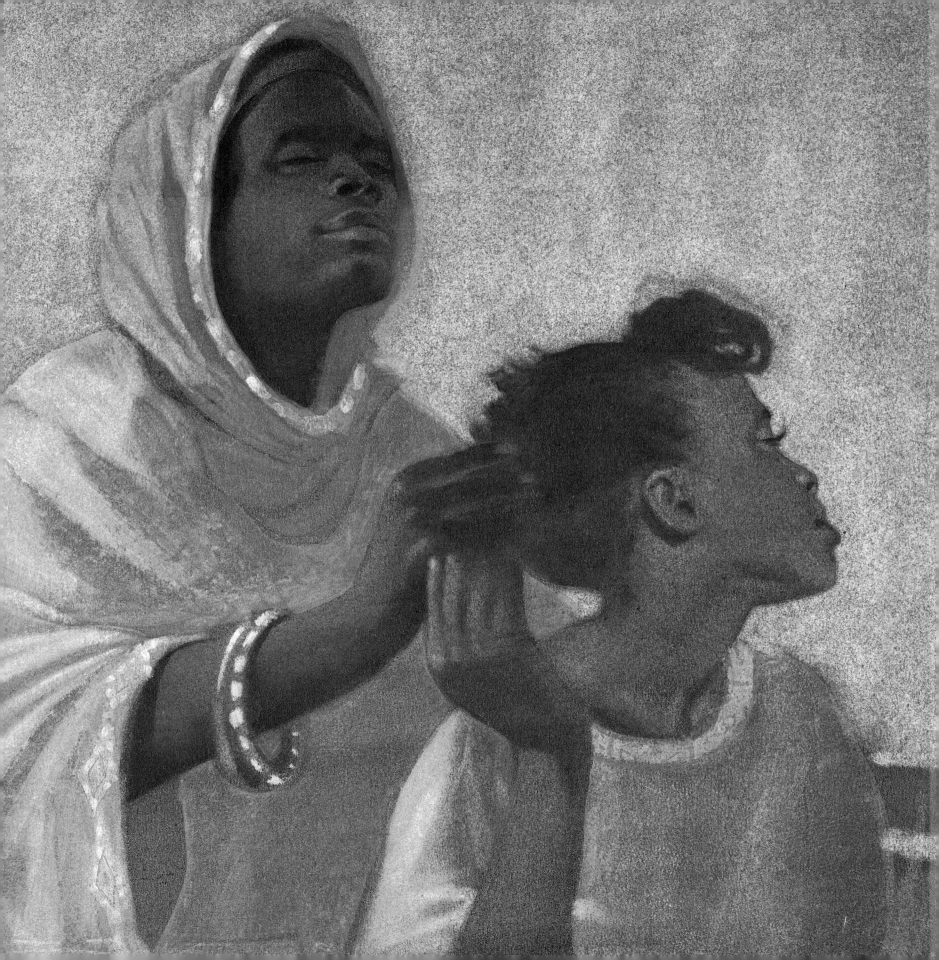

Kibret smiled. "These flowers remind me of my own village," she said. "Come, let me braid your hair for you, and I will show you how to weave the flowers into a crown."

The next morning Almaz ran all the way to her grandfather's hut.

"Sit down," said her grandfather in his silky old voice.

Almaz did a little dance instead.

"Was that your drum I heard in the village yesterday?" he asked.

"Yes," Almaz said. "Yes." She opened her hand and showed him the lion's hair.

"Hah!" he said. "Now you can go home."

"But the secret," Almaz said. "What about the secret?"

Her grandfather smiled. "You yourself have found the secret. Go to your new mother as you did to the lion. Slowly by slowly, a little at a time."

"Oh," Almaz said. "Maybe I have found the secret." She jumped to her feet and rushed out.

Then she stopped. She turned around. "Thank you," she said. She smiled the lion's slow, secret smile and walked slowly home.